LEVEL

N

I'M IN CHARGE OF CELEBRATIONS

by Byrd Baylor / pictures by Peter Parnall

ALADDIN PAPERBACKS

First Aladdin Paperbacks edition October 1995
Text copyright © 1986 Byrd Baylor
Illustrations copyright © 1986 Peter Parnall

Aladdin Paperbacks
An imprint of Simon & Schuster
Children's Publishing Division
1230 Avenue of the Americas
New York, NY 10020

Also available in an Atheneum Books for Young Readers edition

Manufactured in China
30 29 28 27 26 25 24 23 22

The Library of Congress has cataloged the hardcover edition as follows:

Baylor, Byrd.
I'm in charge of celebrations.
Summary: A dweller in the desert celebrates a triple rainbow, a chance
encounter with a coyote, and other wonders of the wilderness.
[1. Deserts—Fiction] I. Parnall, Peter, ill. II. Title.
PZ7.B3435Im 1986
[Fic] 85-19633
ISBN 0-684-18579-2
ISBN 0-689-80620-5 (Aladdin pbk.)

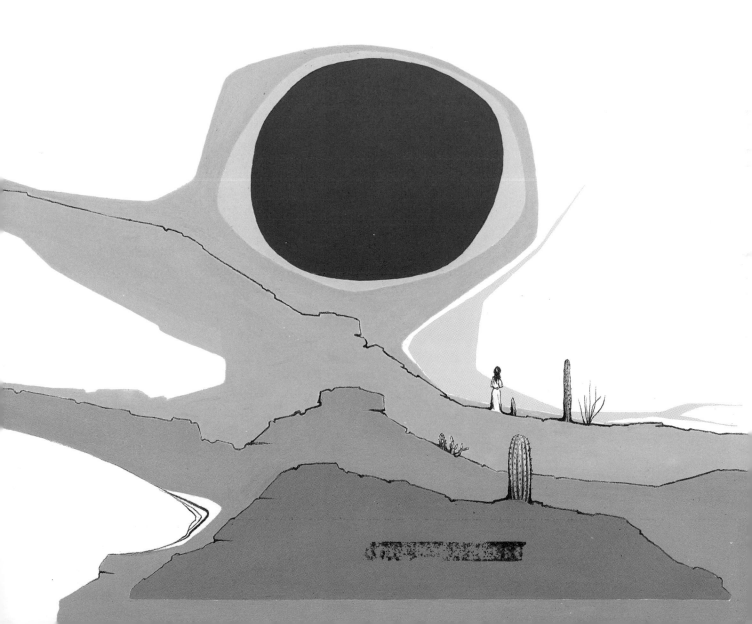

*In celebration of
Leah and Sarah*

Sometimes people ask me,
"Aren't you lonely
out there
with just
desert
around you?"

I guess they mean
the beargrass
and the yuccas
and the cactus
and the rocks.

I guess they mean
the deep ravines
and the hawk nests
in the cliffs
and the coyote trails
that wind
across the hills.

"*Lonely?*"

I can't help
laughing
when they ask me
that.

I always look at them . . .
surprised.

And I say,
"How could I be lonely?
I'm the one
in charge of
celebrations."

Sometimes
they don't believe me,
but it's true.
I am.

I put
myself
in charge.
I choose
my own.

Last year
I gave myself
one hundred and eight
celebrations—
besides the ones
that they close school for.

I cannot get by
with only
a few.

Friend, I'll tell you
how it works.

I keep a notebook
and I write the date
and then I write about
the celebration.

I'm very choosy
over
what goes in
that book.

It has to be something
I plan to remember
the rest of my life.

You can tell
what's worth
a celebration
because
your heart will
POUND
and
you'll feel
like you're standing
on top of a mountain
and you'll
catch your breath
like you were
breathing
some new kind of air.

Otherwise,
I count it just
an average day.
(I told you
I was
choosy.)

Friend, I wish you'd been here
for Dust Devil Day.

But since you weren't,
I'll tell you how
it got to be
my first
real
celebration.

You can call them
whirlwinds
if you want to.
Me, I think
dust devils
has a better sound.

Well, anyway,
I always stop
to watch them.
Here, everyone does.

You know how
they come
from far away,
moving
up from the flats,
swirling
and swaying
and falling
and turning,
picking up sticks
and sand
and feathers
and dry tumbleweeds.

Well, last March eleventh
we were all going somewhere.
I was in the back
of a pickup truck
when the dust devils
started
to gather.

You could see
they were
giants.

You'd swear
they were
calling
their friends
to come too.

And they came—
dancing
in time to
their own
windy music.

We all started counting.
We all started looking
for more.

They stopped that truck
and we turned
around
and around
watching them all.
There were seven.

At a time like that,
something
goes kind of crazy
in you.
You have to run
to meet them,
yelling
all the way.

You have to
whirl around
like you were
one of them,
and you can't stop
until
you're falling down.

And then all day
you think
how
lucky
you were
to be there.

Some of my best
celebrations
are sudden surprises
like that.

If you weren't outside
at that
exact
moment,
you'd miss them.

I spend a lot of time
outside
myself,
looking around.

Once
I saw a triple rainbow
that ended in a canyon
where I'd been
the day before.

I was halfway up a hill
standing
in a drizzle of rain.

It was almost dark
but I wouldn't go in
(because of the rainbows,
of course),
and there
at the top of the hill
a jackrabbit
was standing
up on his hind legs,
perfectly still,
looking straight
at that same
triple
rainbow.

I may be
the only person in the world
who's seen
a rabbit
standing in the mist
quietly watching
three rainbows.

That's worth
a celebration
any time.

I wrote it down
and drew the hill
and the rabbit
and the rainbow
and me.

Now
August ninth
is Rainbow Celebration Day.

I have
Green Cloud Day
too.

Ask anybody
and they'll tell you
clouds
aren't
green.

But
late one winter afternoon
I saw
this huge
green cloud.

It was not
bluish-green
or grayish-green
or something else.
This cloud
was
green . . .

green as a jungle parrot.

And the strange thing was
that it began
to take a parrot's shape,
first
the wings,
and then the head
and beak.

High in the winter sky
that green bird
flew.

It didn't last
more than a minute.
You know how fast
a cloud
can change,
but I still
remember
how it looked.

So I celebrate
green clouds
on February sixth.

At times like that,
I always think,
"What if I'd missed it?
What if I'd been
in the house?
Or what if I hadn't
looked up
when I did?"

You can see I'm
very lucky
about things
like that.

And
I was lucky
on Coyote Day,
because
out of all time
it had to be
one moment
only
that
a certain coyote
and I
could meet—
and we did.

Friend, you should have
been here too.

I was following
deer tracks,
taking my time,
bending down
as I walked,
kind of humming.
(I hum a lot
when I'm alone.)

I looked up
in time to see
a young coyote
trotting
through the brush.

She crossed
in front of me.
It was a windy day
and she was going east.

In that easy
silent way
coyotes move,
she pushed
into the wind.

I stood there
hardly breathing,
wishing I
could move
that way.

I was surprised
to see her
stop
and turn
and look
at me.

She seemed to think
that I was
just
another
creature
following another
rocky trail.

(That's true, of course.
I am.)

She didn't hurry.
She wasn't afraid.

I saw her eyes
and she saw
mine.

That look
held us
together.

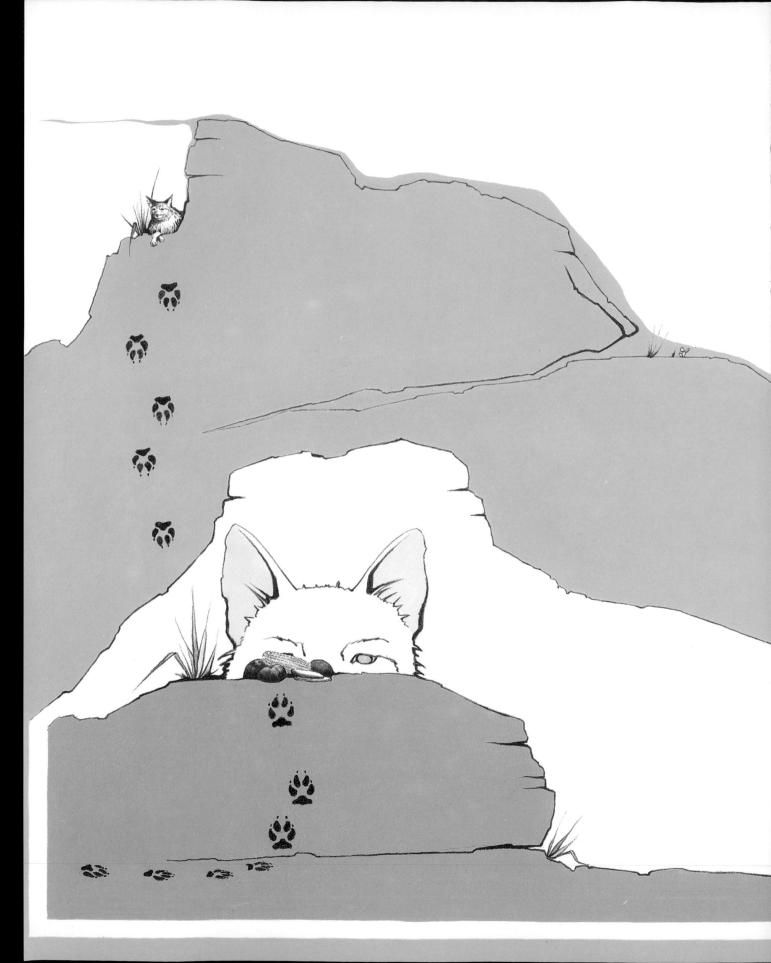

Because of that,
I never will
feel
quite the same
again.

So
on September twenty-eighth
I celebrate
Coyote Day.

Here's what I do:
I walk
the trail
I walked that day,
and I hum
softly
as I go.

Finally,
I unwrap
the feast
I've brought for her.

Last time
it was three apples
and some pumpkin seeds
and an ear of corn
and some big soft homemade
ginger cookies.

The next day,
I happened to pass
that way again.
Coyote tracks
went all around
the rock
where the food had been,
and the food
was gone.

Next year
I'll make it even better.
I'll bring
an extra feast
and eat there too.

Another one
of my greatest
of all celebrations
is called
The Time of Falling Stars.

It lasts
almost a week
in the middle
of August,
and I wait
all year
for those hot
summer nights
when the sky
goes
wild.

You can call them
meteor showers
if you want to.
Me, I like to say
they're
falling stars.

All that week
I sleep outside.

I give
my full attention
to the sky.

And every time
a streak of light
goes
shooting
through the darkness,
I feel my heart
shoot
out of me.

One night
I saw
a fireball
that left
a long
red
blazing
trail
across the sky.

After it was
gone,
I stood there
looking up,
not quite
believing
what I'd seen.

The strange thing was,
I met a man
who told me
he had seen it too
while he was lying
by a campfire
five hundred miles
away.

He said he did not sleep
again
that night.

Suddenly
it seemed
that we two
spoke a language
no one else
could
understand.

Every August
of my life,
I'll think of that.

Friend,
I've saved
my New Year Celebration
until last.

Mine
is a little
different
from the one
most people have.

It comes in
spring.

To tell the truth,
I never did
feel like
my new year
started
January first.

To me,
that's just
another
winter day.

I let my year
begin
when winter
ends
and morning light
comes
earlier,
the way it *should*.

That's when
I feel like
starting
new.

I wait
until
the white-winged doves
are back from Mexico,
and wildflowers
cover the hills,
and my favorite
cactus
blooms.

It always
makes me think
I ought to bloom
myself.

And
that's when
I start to plan
my New Year
celebration.

I finally choose
a day
that is
exactly
right.

Even the air
has to be
perfect,
and the dirt
has to feel
good and warm
on bare feet.

(Usually,
it's a Saturday
around the end
of April.)

I have a drum
that I beat
to signal
The Day.

Then I go
wandering off,
following all
of my favorite
trails
to all of the
places
I like.

I check how
everything
is doing.

I spend the day
admiring
things.

If the old desert tortoise
I know from last year
is out
strolling around,
I'll go his direction
awhile.

I celebrate
with horned toads
and ravens
and lizards
and quail . . . .

And, Friend,
it's not
a bad
party.

Walking back home
(kind of humming),
sometimes
I think about
those people
who ask me if
I'm *lonely* here.

I have to
laugh
out
loud.

Byrd Baylor and Peter Parnall
have collaborated on three Calde-
cott Honor books: *The Desert Is
Theirs*; *Hawk, I'm Your Brother*; and
The Way to Start a Day.

Byrd Baylor lives in the South-
west. Her eloquent lyric prose
reflects a philosophy as special
and lovely as the lands she writes
about. For her it is the spirit — not
material things — that is necessary
for personal development. "Once
you make that decision, your
whole life opens up and you begin
to know what matters and what
doesn't."

Peter Parnall lives on a farm in
Maine with his wife and two children. His drawings have been
described as stunning, glittering
and breathtaking. When he draws
the animal world, he has an
uncanny ability to portray that
world as the animals themselves
might experience it.